First Day of School

Judy Nayer

illustrated by Jason Wolff

SCHOLASTIC INC.
New York Toronto London Auckland Sydney
Mexico City New Delhi Hong Kong Buenos Aires

To all good things
—J. N.

For Shawn, Jan, Abby, and Callie,
with love
—J. W.

ISBN-13: 978-0-545-09889-2
ISBN-10: 0-545-09889-0

Text copyright © 2008 by Judy Nayer
Illustrations copyright © 2008 by Jason Wolff
All rights reserved. Published by Scholastic Inc. SCHOLASTIC,
The Lunch Bunch™, and associated logos are trademarks and/or
registered trademarks of Scholastic Inc.

Lexile is a registered trademark of MetaMetrics, Inc.

12 11 10 9 8 7 6 5 4 3 2 1   8 9 10 11 12 13/0

Printed in the U.S.A.
First printing, September 2008

Book design by Nancy Sabato-Martin

The First Day

My name is Matt.

Today I start first grade!

I am ready.

I have my new cap.

I have my new sneakers.

I have my new backpack.

"Ready, Matt?" asks Mom.

"Yes!" I say.

"WAH! WAH! WAH!"

"Hmmm. Ben is not ready,"

says Mom.

Ben is my baby brother.

He cries a lot.

Mom says all babies cry a lot.

I know what to do.

I take off my cap.

I cover my face.

I take away my cap.

"Peek-a-boo!" I say.

Ben stops crying.

I do it again.

"Peek-a-boo!" I say.

Ben is smiling!

Now we are ready.

Mom pushes Ben down the block.

She is singing and smiling.

Mom smiles a lot.

Even if something bad happens,

she smiles.

"It's okay! It's all good!" she says.

"Look, Mom! There they are!" I say.

"Kate! Sam! Jen!" I call.

They are my three best friends.

We all live on the same block.

We have been friends

since we were babies.

Kate and Sam and Jen and I

do everything together.

We went to preschool together.

We went to camp together.

We went to kindergarten together.

Now we are going to first grade

together!

"Hi, Matt!" they say.

"Ready for the first day?" I ask.

"Yes!" says Kate.

"Yup!" says Sam.

"Yeah!" says Jen.

Now I am smiling.

First grade is going to be the best!

A Bad Surprise

We go into school.

"Look!" says Kate. "That list says

Room 102. It has our names on it."

I love lists.

I love words, too.

I read the list.

It has Kate's name.

It has Sam's name.

It has Jen's name.

It does not have my name.

"Matt!" says Sam.

"*There* is your name!"

My name is on the list

that says Room 104.

"Oh, no!" I say.

Kate and Sam and Jen are

in the same class.

But I am not!

This is bad.

There must be a mistake.

But there isn't.

It's just bad.

Really, really, really, really bad.

I'm not smiling anymore.

I feel terrible.

First grade is not the best.

It's the worst!

Even Mom doesn't say,

"It's okay! It's all good!"

She says, "I'm sorry.

I know this is bad.

But there will be good things

about first grade, too.

You'll see."

I don't think so.

Kate and Sam and Jen and I

do everything together.

How can I go to first grade

without them?

Kate and Sam and Jen go into

Room 102.

"Goodbye, Matt," they say.

"Goodbye," I say.

I feel sad.

I feel like I just lost my best friends.

Wait a minute!

I *did* just lose my best friends!

Room 104

My new teacher is at the door.

"Hi!" she says, smiling.

"I am Miss Gold.

What is your name?"

"Matt," I say.

"It's nice to meet you, Matt.

I like your backpack!"

"Thanks," I say.

"Your teacher seems nice," says Mom.

"I'll see you later.

Don't forget. Look for the good things.

You will feel better."

Miss Gold tells me to look for my seat.

I try to be brave.

I go into Room 104 and find my seat.

I am at a table with two girls and a boy.

I wish those two girls and a boy were Kate and Jen and Sam.

I can read the boy's name. It is Max.

"Hi, Matt!" he says.

I guess he can read my name, too.

"We have the best seats in first

grade," says Max.

"We are right next to the hamster.

His name is Harry."

Max is right.

Harry the hamster is so close

we can touch his cage.

Max pokes his pencil in.

He makes the wheel turn.

Harry hops on and runs.

"Cool!" I say.

I poke my finger in.

Harry runs over and sniffs it.

Miss Gold comes over.

I think she is going to be mad.

But she is still smiling.

"Harry likes you!" she says.

Boy, she is nice!

Next Miss Gold takes *attendance*.

This is new in first grade.

The teacher says your name.

You raise your hand and say, "Here!"

"Matt," says Miss Gold, "I have a job for you. Take this list and go to Room 102. Get Mr. Bard's list. Then take both lists to the office. Can you do all that?"

"I think so!" I say.

This is great!

I get to go to Room 102!

I take the list.

It's a nice list.

Miss Gold has neat writing.

I go across the hall to Room 102.

I see Kate and Sam and Jen!

"Matt!" they yell.

"Hush!" yells Mr. Bard.

"May I help you?" he asks.

Mr. Bard is not smiling.

Mr. Bard looks like he *never* smiles.

I'm too scared to talk.

I get the list and go. Fast.

The hall is *soooooo* long.

It's like Mr. Bard—a little scary.

At last I make it to the office.

When I get back to Room 104,

Miss Gold is still smiling.

"Good job, Matt!" she says.

I feel good.

This must be one of the good things.

It's time for reading.

Max is my reading buddy.

We read a book about sharks.

It's really cool.

Max is nice.

He's not Sam, who is my best,

best friend.

But he's pretty cool.

Next we have math.

Miss Gold puts a jelly bean into a jar.

I love jelly beans.

"Yum!" I say.

"I'll put a jelly bean into the jar

every day," says Miss Gold.

"When we get to 100, the first grade

will have a party!"

All this talk about jelly beans makes

me hungry.

Then Miss Gold reads a story.

It's *really* funny.

All kinds of food drops from the sky.

Now I am really hungry.

Miss Gold must know

what I'm thinking.

The next thing she says is,

"Okay, boys and girls,

it's time for lunch!"

The Lunch Bunch

I walk into the lunchroom.

"MATT!" yell Kate and Sam and Jen.

"Over here!"

They are sitting at a table.

I go over.

"Good news!" says Kate.

"You can sit anywhere in first grade."

"You mean we can eat together?" I ask.

"Yup!" says Sam.

"Every day?" I say.

"Yeah, every day," says Jen.

"Promise?" I ask.

"YES!" they say.

"Let's eat!" says Kate.

"I have ham," I say.

"I have ham, too," says Kate.

"I have turkey," says Sam.

"I have cheese," says Jen.

"Let's mix," we say.

We all have ham and turkey and cheese sandwiches.

We may not be in the same class, but Kate and Sam and Jen and I can eat lunch together!

This is really, really good!

I tell them about the jelly bean jar.

"We don't have jelly beans,"

says Kate.

I tell them about my seat

near Harry the hamster.

"We don't even have a hamster,"

says Sam.

I tell them about the funny book

Miss Gold read.

"Mr. Bard read a story," says Kate.

"Yeah," says Jen,

"but it wasn't funny."

"There's *nothing* funny

about Mr. Bard," says Sam.

"I have an idea," I say.

"Let's eat together every day."

"We already said that," says Jen.

"I mean, let's really promise," I say.

"Let's start a club."

"Good idea!" says Kate.

"Let's call it *The Lunch Bunch*!"

"I like it!" says Jen.

"Me, too!" I say.

"Yup!" says Sam.

"Great!" says Kate, "but let's *go*.

We don't want to miss recess."

Recess!

I almost forgot!

Kate and Sam and Jen and I

can play together at recess!

Recess is the best.

First we play tag.

Then we play kickball.

Then we go on the jungle gym.

It's just like old times.

Except for Max.

"Hi!" I say. "You're a good climber!"

"Thanks!" he says.

Kate and Sam and Jen think Max

is pretty cool.

When the bell rings, I'm sad.

I want to go with my friends

into Room 102.

Maybe I can sneak in.

Maybe there is an empty seat.

I peek in.

There isn't an empty seat.

There's just Mr. Bard.

And he's still not smiling.

I look over at Room 104.

There's Miss Gold, smiling.

"See you later!" I wave

to Kate and Sam and Jen.

As I take my seat,

I make a list in my head.

Miss Gold tells us about

the Word Wall.

"If you learn a new word you can

write it on a card. Then you can put

the card on the Word Wall."

Since I love words, I love this idea.

I want to think of a really, really,

really, good word.

"Can my word for the Word Wall

be more than one word?" I ask.

"Sure," says Miss Gold.

"What do you have in mind?"

"Today I started a club," I say.

"It's called *The Lunch Bunch*."

Miss Gold gives me a card.

I write *The.*

Miss Gold writes *Lunch.*

I write *Bunch.*

"Excellent!" says Miss Gold.

At the End of the Day

I see my friends come out of school.

"Kate! Sam! Jen!" I yell.

"Hi, Matt!" they yell back.

"Mr. Bard gave us homework,"

says Sam.

"Do you have homework?" asks Jen.

"No," I say.

"Miss Gold says this week
we should just play."

"Wow!" says Kate. "She sounds
really nice."

"She is," I say.

"Hi, Mom!" I say.

"Hi!" says Mom. "How was it?"

"You were right," I say. "There are some good things about first grade."

"Great!" says Mom. "Let's go home and you can tell me."

Kate and Sam and Jen and I

walk home together.

But they have homework.

"Goodbye!" I say. "Don't forget!

The Lunch Bunch meets at my

house in one hour."

Mom tapes a big sheet of paper

on my door.

"I know what that's for!" I say.

It's the paper we use for lists.

We have been writing lists

since I was little.

I think that is why I love lists

so much.

Once, when I was potty training,

we made a list of all the bathrooms

I went to.

Another time, we made a list of

things to put in a magic potion.

At the top of the paper, Mom writes,

WHY I LIKE FIRST GRADE

"OK, Matt," she says.

"Tell me the good things!"

First I think about the bad thing.

That is big.

But then I start to think of the

good things.

Soon I have a nice list going.

WHY I LIKE FIRST GRADE

Miss Gold

My seat

Harry the Hamster

Taking the attendance lists
to the office

Max, my reading buddy and
new friend

A funny read-aloud book

The jelly bean jar

Lunch (with my friends!)

The Lunch Bunch club

Recess (with my friends!)

Word Wall

Harry the Hamster

Taking the attendance lists to the office

Max, my reading buddy and new friend

A funny read-aloud book

The jelly bean jar

Lunch (with my friend

The Lunch Bunch

Recess (with my

Word Wall

I read over the whole list.

I like it.

It is a good list.

There are a lot of good things on it.

I bet there will be more.

First grade is looking better already.